Mommy is that you?

Atsuko Morozumi

E MOROZUMI
Morozumi, Atsuko,
Mommy is that you? /

MATHEW PRICE LIMITED

PALM BEACH COUNTY
LIBRARY SYSTEM
3650 Summit Boulevard
West Palm Beach, FL 33406-4198

Mrs. Duck had four eggs in her little house under the willow tree. One blowy day a gust of wind picked up her house and threw it high into the air.

The nest flew in the wind
till it landed on someone's back

... with a PLONK!

The eggs cracked open and four
little ducklings were born.

"Hello," they said. "Are you our Mommy?"

"Certainly not," said the tortoise.

So the ducklings set off to find their Mommy. First they met someone soft and fluffy.

"Are you our
Mommy?"
they asked.

"Dear me, no," growled the dog.

The ducklings
left in a hurry.

The four little ducklings
were just having a rest, when
somebody walked by with lots of
little babies just like them.
"She must be Mommy," they cried.

"I'm sorry," said the hen, "but I'm not your Mommy."

Next the ducklings came to a pond. Someone was splashing about in the water. "Are you our Mommy?" they called out.

"You must be joking," said the fish,
as she swam away.

The ducklings decided to have a swim too.

They were happily splashing about when one of them swam smack into a white, fluffy back. "Quackety quack, what's that?" a voice said.

A lovely duck turned around,
looking at them all with a
big smile.
"Mommy!"

Mrs. Duck took her ducklings home. Their little house was back in its place underneath the willow tree. This time it was tied fast with a great big rope.

The End